My Feelings and Body

FROM ADVENTURES IN FRIENDSHIP TOWN
with MUSHY, THE MAGIC BOOK

CREATED AND WRITTEN BY
AVA PARNASS, WITH REBECCA PARNASS
ILLUSTRATED BY AL MARGOLIS

Ava Parnass MSN, a Child and Family Psychotherapist with over 15 years of experience, has developed a series of fun, interactive projects for children that also encourage emotional health. A published songwriter and author, she has collaborated on various projects since 1998 with some of New York's most prominent talents.

To hear Mushy's theme song, "Gotta Find Out", visit www.listentomeplease.com

Rebecca Parnass has been singing, creating books and movies since she was 4 years old.

Al Margolis is well known for his inventive visuals and insightful, humorous illustrations. His career includes a long stint as an advertising agency art director, and more recently as owner of Margolis Creative, a graphic design and illustration group.

His clients have included a children's art center, a private school, foster care and adoption home, and a special needs facility. Helping children enjoy, learn and understand their experiences is an important part of his work. He brings his broad experience and supportive approach to every project.

To see more of his work visit www.almargolis.com

LOVE AND THANKS TO:

TAL, REBECCA, ALEX FORBES, AL MARGOLIS, KATE KAMINSKI, RENEE SCHLESINGER, ROBIN COREY, STEPHANIE GOLDMAN, TERRY SILVERLIGHT, GILBERT CHIROPRACTIC (MERCEDES, DANA, MILLE, FRANK, ANGELA), WONDERFUL SISTER ITA, EXCELLENT BROTHERS DR. SAM, DR. MARK, LOVING FAMILY: CARYL, MARGOT, JUDI, LAURA, DANI, ADAM, EITAN, BELLA, TALEAH. LISA, ARI, NOAH, LAURIE, LINDSAY, AMY, DORA, YAEL, GILI, NANCY, ALLIE, JORDAN, AUDREY, CAROLINE, DANA, HALLEY, JULIE, JEREMY. A SPECIAL THANKS TO MY LOVING, GENEROUS PARENTS, NORMAN AND AGNES PARNASS

ISBN: 1-4392-0352-0   ISBN 13: 9781439203521   ©2008 Ava Parnass   Published in the USA
Library of Congress catalog card number 2008906442

Let me tell you the tale of one Very Bad Day
It's a bit unbelievable, that's what you'll say
It all started at school, and got worse all day long
Good thing Mushy my friend helps me fix what goes wrong!

When I got home that day there was trouble in store
Threw my coat on the chair, and my books on the floor
"Rebecca!" my grown-ups yelled, "stop it right now,
Don't keep slamming that door shut, you know it's too loud!"

My grown-ups told somebody else "I love you"
Do they know how I missed them? Do they love me too?
I kicked over my toy box and stomped on the ground
Then went straight for the candy, to help me calm down

I had cupcakes and chocolate and chips up to here
Then I washed it all down with a bunch of root beer
I hid under the bed to gulp down some ice cream
If I didn't keep eating, I'd just want to scream!

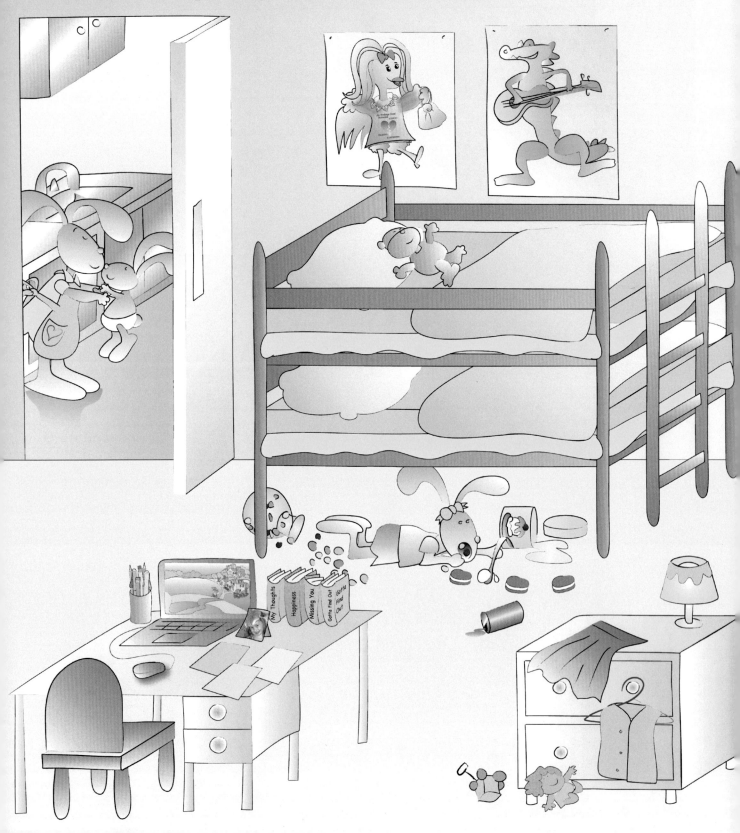

Nobody asked me, and I couldn't say
Was there something that made me so hungry that day?
My grown-ups had said "you'll cheer up if you eat"
But then they said "stop it, that's too many sweets!"

Can't somebody bring me a great magic wand
That could make all these big hungry feelings be gone?
I ran straight to my room, I was still feeling weird
And turned on my computer... then Mushy appeared!

She's a magical book that you'll all want to see
And she's full of ideas and adventures for me
First she froze all the grown-ups with her magic spell
Then she made ice cubes out of the words that they yelled

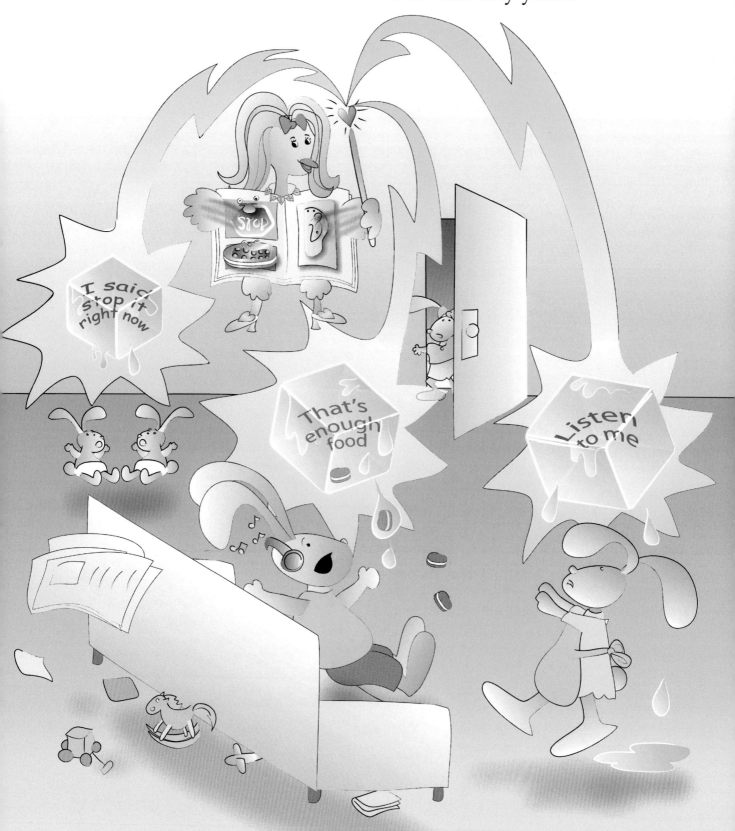

We flew into the sky in her cool E-Mobile
Off to Feeling Town, where kids find out what they feel
Mushy helps me explain, when my feelings get hurt
So I don't need to eat all that extra dessert!

There's a bright-colored school in the middle of town
Mushy's just like a tour guide, she showed me around:

"Over here is our blackboard,
except this one's pink

Pick a picture that paints how you feel

And a pool of blue tears
makes a great skating rink!"

And then Mushy threw open the book on her chest
Asking "Which color feeling would fit you the best?"

Were you blue?
Yellow? Purple? Excited? Annoyed?
Did you want be perfect, or break all your toys?"

So I picked out the picture that seemed right to me
Then we walked through the neighborhood — so much to see!
Every street had the name of a feeling I've had
The up, down and sideways ones, happy and sad

There's Lonely Lane, Silly Street, Jealousy Road
If you turn green with envy, then that's where you go
Hungry Hollow's for children who eat and can't stop
The streetlights are pizzas, with mushrooms on top!

Watch your temper whenever you're on Tantrum Trail
All the kids run in circles, they cry and they wail
You might want some earplugs to block out the noise
Or slip over to Silent Street if that's your choice

I looked over at Love Street, and said, "Mushy, please?
That's where sweet hugs and kisses are growing on trees!"
But another sign pointed to Very Bad Days
In the end Hungry Hollow's the choice that I made

Mushy told me that asking for so many treats
Means I'm not saying something I feel underneath
So I told her what happened one step at a time
Like a tangled-up string that I had to unwind

My friend Tal was ignoring me, that made me sad
Then when Allie made fun of me, that got me mad!
Lindsay stopped me from singing — she wanted to play
But I sing when I'm happy or when I'm afraid

When my grown-up was yelling, now that was the worst
I was angry and jealous and ready to burst!
I wondered if anyone loved me at all
Mushy said "what's the very first thing you recall?"

Thinking back, it all started when I left for school
I was feeling so lonely, but acted so cool
Like a snake-bite, a boo-boo, a big broken heart (an ouchie, an owie)
Those goodbyes made my very good day fall apart

Then we jumped in the E-Mobile, and flew through the sky
Mushy said that my very bad day would rewind!
We could have a do-over and unfreeze those words
And I'd soon be un-lonely, un-hungry, un-hurt

My do-over with Tal meant he did want to play
And then Allie said, "Sorry I acted that way"
Lindsay told me "I love you, your singing is dreamy"
Those words were much sweeter than anything creamy

See, it wasn't my tummy that needed some food
When my feelings are hungry, there's one thing to do:
Find somebody to listen, and hear what's inside
Then whatever went wrong, it can start to go right

My grown-ups sat down on the edge of my bed
And I'm sure that they heard every word that I said
There were tears and some smiles, then a kiss on my cheek
Mushy whispered "it looks like you're on Happy Street!"

That's when all of the junk food I wanted before
Didn't seem half as yummy to me any more
'Cause no cookie, no candy, no marvelous meal
Only listening to me will fix what I feel

THANK YOU MUSHY! YOU HELP WHEN MY FEELINGS GET HURT.
WHEN THEY LISTEN TO ME...THAT'S THE PERFECT DESSERT!

Grab the hand of your grown-up and sit in their lap
Pick a face, then your place on the Feeling Town map
Are you up, down or sideways? Need a hug or a kiss?
Is there someone you're mad at, or someone you miss?

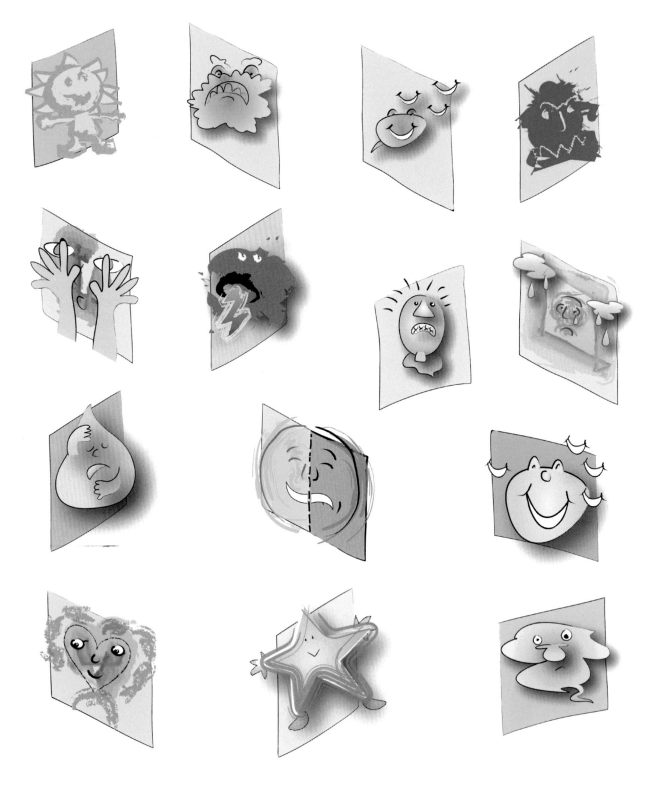

HERO'S PLAYGROUND

NEVER GIVE UP

HOPE ROAD

WHINING HILL

I FIGURE OUT HOW I FEEL

COMPASSIONATE PLACE

SMART AND CURIOUS ROAD

JOY ROAD

HOPELESS RIVER

GO GET HELP STREET

COPING MEADOW

HEALING LANE

CONFIDENCE ROAD

HURT FEELINGS HOLLOW

BORING BOULEVARD

I TELL THE TRUTH STREET

HUGS AND KISSES CORNER

SHY LANE

A VERY GOOD DAY STREET

LOVE STREET

LAUGHING HYSTERICALLY LANE

GLUE MY FEELINGS BACK TOGETHER

HAPPY STREET

MISTAKE STREET

SORRY LANE

BROKEN HEARTED LANE (AN OUCHIE, AN OWIE)

TOO HARD TO SAY

FABULOUS STREET

EMERGENCY BATHROOM STREET

COMPLIMENTS

CONFUSED AND FRUSTRATED HILL

FISHING FOR COMPLIMENTS

SILENT STREET

LISTEN TO ME PLEASE

JEALOUSY ROAD

KIND WORDS STREET

NAME A NEW STREET

LOOSE TOOTH STREET

I FEEL SAD WHEN YOU LEAVE

"GIVE ME" STREET

PERSISTENCE AND PATIENCE STREET

FEELINGS CENTER

BOOK STORE

I MISS YOU HILL

IMAGINATION STREET

BULLY LANE

TANTRUM TRAIL

ANGRY STREET

SAD STREET

LUCKY TO HAVE YOU STREET

SCARED HOLLOW

HYPER AND I CAN'T SIT STILL

DECLARATION OF FEELINGS AVENUE

HUNGRY HOLLOW

NEW FRIENDS AVENUE

BRAVE ROAD

SHARING STREET

EXCITED AND SURPRISE ROAD

VERY BAD DAY STREET

LONELY LANE

EXERCISE AND RELAXING LANE

"TIL I TALK ABOUT HOW I FEEL AVENUE

I HELP MYSELF AND OTHERS MEADOW

DISAPPOINTED ROAD

I WISH STREET

I FEEL BETTER AND GET OVER IT STREET

SHUSH UP AVENUE

WELCOME TO FEELING TOWN

IT'S OK TO BE MYSELF

SILLY STREET

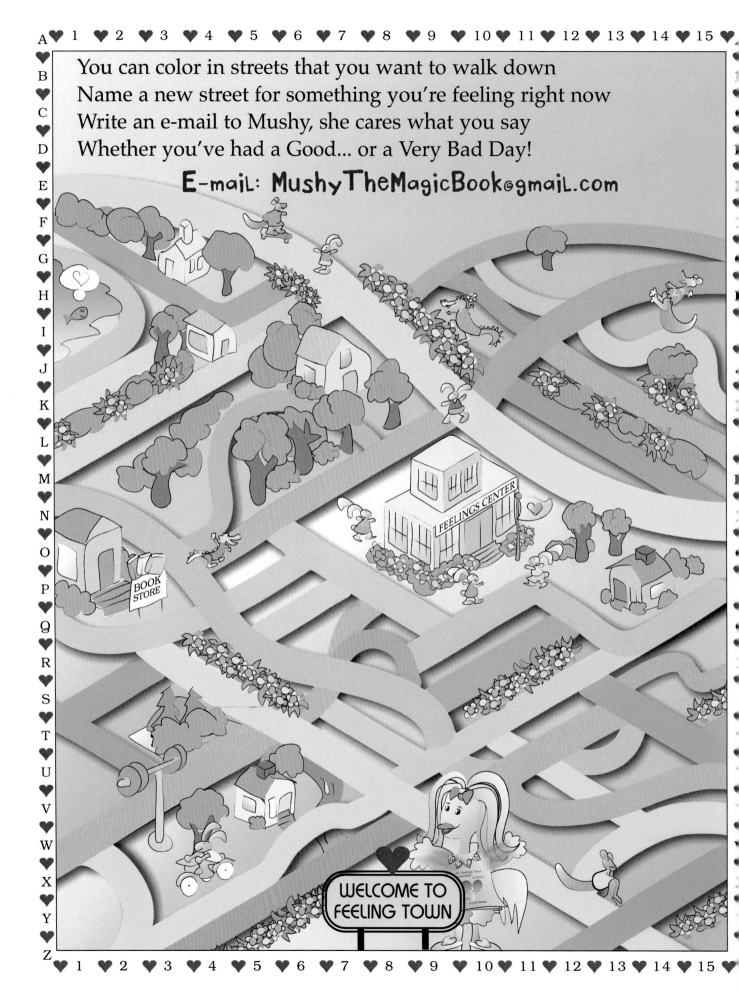

You can color in streets that you want to walk down
Name a new street for something you're feeling right now
Write an e-mail to Mushy, she cares what you say
Whether you've had a Good... or a Very Bad Day!

E-mail: MushyTheMagicBook@gmail.com

Made in the USA
Middletown, DE
16 November 2017